Living and Loving Wrong

Stephanie Diane

Published by Stephanie Diane
© 2019, Stephanie Diane

Although this book was inspired by actual events and real people, certain characters portrayed, characterizations, scenes and dialogue spoken represent a work of dramatic fiction.

ISBN-13 978-0-578-61559-2

First Printing, December 2019

10 9 8 7 6 5 4 3 2 1

Dedication

"To my children whom I love whole heartedly. Keep your life free from the love of money and be content with what you have.

For he has said,
"I will never leave you nor forsake you"
Hebrews 13:5

Acknowledgements

First and foremost, I want give thanks to my almighty God, without you none of this would be possible.

I want to thank my children, without you all I wouldn't know what strength is. I want to take this opportunity to say I'm sorry for all the mistakes that I have made while raising you all. I became a mother when I was just a child myself. There was no handbook for how to be a parent. All I could offer was my unconditional love but I don't regret having you all. You all saved my life.

Marquavis my first born having you changed my life completely and I'm forever grateful you have such a pure heart and you are the best big brother ever. I will never forget how you picked up the slack. I just want to thank you.

Rakajah continue being the ambitious and adventurous young lady you are. Your drive makes me so proud.

Yasin, my miracle baby I will never forget the day you were born. The doctors gave up, but I didn't, and I never will. I dropped to my knees and prayed to God to keep you alive. I knew you were a survivor. You are the strongest most stern person I know.

Kaleese, don't give up on that nursing degree I can't wait to see you cross that stage. The determination you have is well worth it.

Niya J, my sweet baby girl you're such a smart and influential person continue to stay focus you doing such a great job.

Messiah my comedian if you only knew how your personality keeps me going on my bad days. I just know you will be a famous comedian one day.

Last but not least my K.J, your smile is everything to me your sweet little spirit brightens up every room.

I just want y'all to know I'm so proud of each and every one of you and I love y'all. Remember one for all and all for one.

Ma, there is no way I could pay you back in three lifetimes for what you have done for my children and I. I just want you to know I appreciate you without you it would be no me. You are the GOAT (greatest of all times) I love you ma.

To my aunt Diane may you continue to rest in peace. I hope you are proud of me. I love you.

To my love what can I say but wow! You are everything I prayed for and more. The love I have for you is unimaginable. Bae, I love how you inspire me to be a better me. I love how you love and care for my children. You are the best father our boys could have. It takes a real man to do that and baby that's exactly who you are, a real man. I love you Mr. Kelvin Dunn.

To my dad, thank you for all you have done for me. I love you.

To my brothers, I love y'all.

To my uncle Tony, The realest O.G who has ever lived. Rest in Peace. I love you.

To my cousins Shadonna and Bre, we go back like four flat tires. I love ya'll.

To my friends more like sisters Crystal, Tish, Esha, Patricia, Cindy and Krystal, I'm forever thankful for y'all. I love y'all.

To my entire family I love y'all.

"If Loving you is wrong, I don't want to be right" a line we've all heard before. There was a time in my life I shared Luther Ingram's exact sentiments, not only was I loving the wrong man, I didn't even love myself and it spilled over into the way I lived.

I was living wrong and doing all the wrong things. I mean we were all living and loving wrong, my family, my friends and me.

We didn't have a clue on how to get it right.

I thought I knew what love was and how to love the ones around me, I gave them every ounce of me. I made sacrifices hoping to never lose their love. I thought I cracked the code on the good life when the abundance of money started flowing in,I quickly realized I may have had a lot of money, but my life was anything but good. I was tired of loving wrong, I was tired of living wrong, I wanted to get it right. It was time I got it right.

Chapter 1

Losing Love

As far back as I can remember, I saw the people around me living and loving wrong. Loving the wrong people and living the wrong life. It was the norm for them, and it soon would become the norm for me.
I was born on April 13,1978 in Warrenton, North Carolina a small town outside of Raleigh North Carolina filled with tobacco fields and fireflies, Warrenton was home. My parents named me Lauren.

Life was simple when I was younger. My parents met when my mother was fourteen and my dad was nineteen.

They were high school sweethearts. They got married and a few years later my brother was born and soon after I followed. Although they loved one another and my father provided a decent home, over the years my mother felt smothered in that marriage and decided to seek another relationship outside of him.

They were already having issues and being that my mother found comfort in another man, they decided it was best to go their separate ways. We left my dad in Warrenton and my mother moved us to Rocky Mount, North Carolina a country town a little bigger than Warrenton. I was five years old at the time and the split took a toll on me, I felt like I was losing my dad and my brother all at the same time.

My dad decided it was best I go live with my mom and it was best for my brother to live with him. He figured he couldn't do anything with me, and that girls need their mother. I had no choice but to go live with her. She packed me up, dragging me all the way to the car as I screamed for my dad and my brother Paul.

My tears couldn't help me, my dad picked me up and strapped me in the car, he kissed me on the forehead and closed the door. The tears never stopped.

My mom revved the engine and pulled out of the driveway. I put my hand out the window, Paul was crying and yelling "Please don't take my sister, please don't take my sister", my brother who was once close, was now far away from me. I cried all the way to my new home.

My dad did what he did best, he provided me with many things except for his time. He would come to see me occasionally on the weekends. Although they were few and far between, anytime with my dad I cherished. My favorite thing to do was to go to the dollar movies, my dad would let me get whatever I wanted. You couldn't tell me nothing, whatever type of candy I saw, is the type of candy I got. I would eat so much; I'd often give myself a stomachache. Those were the best times, and I craved for more days like that, but I couldn't help but feel like I lost a bit of his love when we moved away. My dad hardly showed any emotions, so it was hard to tell just how much he loved me.

Life with my mother was good, she was what they called a go getter. She was a hustler and made it happen for me and my brother. She owned a cleaning service and a daycare. She also played "Cards" which was another one of her many hustles, she would also send me to her friend Joyce's house to put her numbers in. I remember her always writing them down to make sure I didn't forget them. I watched my mom, give us the world. It was nothing she wouldn't do for us. We lived a good life until her boyfriend decided he wanted to make her his personal punching bag.

I grew tired of having to jump in to save her. This was normal for them, fighting one day and kissing the next. I knew my mother wasn't happy and every time he put his hand to her face, he was stripping her away from herself and me and me and my brother.

I was losing my mother but thankfully my grandmother and aunt lived next door and I could run to my aunt for any and everything. She was like a second mother to me and I needed her more than she knew.

She was the first person to ever call me pretty and she would sneak and let me wear red lipstick. She treated me like her little best friend, and she was there for me those times my parents couldn't be. I was glad to have her love.

As the years went on life was getting better my mother finally left her significant other. I was still going with my dad for my routine summer visits. This summer in particular, the summer of '89, was a summer that would forever be etched in my head. I was excited to spend the summer with the people I loved the most and the extra bonus was having my best friend Shermaine spend two weeks with us. Shermaine was my best friend, she was like the sister I never had.

We met in the 4th grade during recess while playing hopscotch. She was new to the school, I instantly welcomed her letting her know she could play with me anytime and from that day forward we were stuck like glue. Shermaine had beautiful chocolate skin, dark like the night and she was just a little taller than me. She had long black hair, that her mother kept relaxed. She was beautiful.

Her family struggled a bit financially, she grew up with very little and her mother often worked two jobs just to make ends meet.

We were polar opposites. I wanted for nothing, my parents may not have always been there as far as time, but they spoiled us financially. Shermaine loved spending time with me because she knew she would be spoiled right along with me.

We spent that summer with my dad in the Tobacco fields riding around with him to pick up Tobacco Hands. They helped pick the Tobacco. We loved it and sometimes we'd just let our hair down and run through the fields, letting the heat of the sun run across our faces. We enjoyed one another and we were living the good life, my dad gave us whatever our hearts desired.

I just knew this was going to be the best summer of my life, I recall laying on the floor in the living room watching Michael Jordan in the finals when my dad received a phone call from my mother informing him that my aunt was killed.

The sound of the t.v was faint, and my ears couldn't stop ringing. Time had frozen, and my body hit the floor.

I couldn't lose her, she was like a mother to me. I couldn't lose her love. I later found out her boyfriend beat her and crashed their car leaving her for dead. I was broken after I lost my aunt, she was the only one who showed me love in actions.

My relationship with my parents shifted and I felt myself drifting from them. My dad stopped coming by, he would send his love through the phone and my mother was busy trying to pick up the pieces of her life, she had to give that love to herself.

This type of living and this type of loving was the norm for me, it became a part of my DNA.

Chapter 2

Looking for Love

The years flew by in no time. I went from going to tobacco fields and riding four wheelers to shopping for bras. I was fourteen and I was smelling myself as the old folks would say. I wanted to do what I wanted, when I wanted, and nobody could tell me a thing. I was boy crazy and the boys was crazy about me. I enjoyed the attention and reveled at the fact that these boys would do anything to be with me. It was the way I looked that had them fighting for a place in my life. I didn't even know I possessed this type of beauty until the boys started sniffing around. They fell in love with my almond brown skin, long curly hair, hazel eyes and my big cornbread fed booty.

I had a couple of boyfriends at my school who I thought I loved but those relationships were short lived when they realized I wasn't giving up my virginity.

I wanted to be in love, I wanted a boy to call my own. I wanted to find that love that I felt like I lost all those years ago.

It was a rainy morning and I was on my way to the bus stop. I was dressed in a pair of baggy blue jean overalls with a pink mid-drift shirt underneath. I pulled my curly hair into a low ponytail and I accessorized with three gold necklaces and my large bamboo earrings. I looked good that morning and I just knew some boy was going to try to get with me that day. Little did I know it was going to be the boy who would change my life forever.

The rain started to let up and I was a few feet away from the bus stop, I notice this black car fly past me, it quickly put on brakes and made a U-turn right in the middle of the street. The car pulled up on the side of me and I noticed there were a few guys inside the car. The driver yelled out the window.

"Hey sexy!".

"Are you talking to me?" I inquired.

"Yea sexy, so what's up?"

"My name isn't sexy!" I shot back rolling my eyes so hard, they could've popped out of my head.

"My bad baby, what's your name then?" the driver asked.

I ignored his inquiry and kept walking towards the bus stop. He jumped out of the car and followed behind me.

"Can I get your number?"

I shook my head no.

"You gonna do me like that, let me get to know you, what's it gonna hurt you givin' me yo number?" He begged.

I wasn't going to give him my number, but the bus finally arrived, and he wouldn't leave me alone. I gave him my number and my name. He said his name was David, but his boys call him "D".

"Ima call you later!" he yelled as I stepped on the bus.

He was a man of his word and called me as soon as I got home from school. We talked for hours on the phone that day and the days that followed. He was funny and he was smart, and not to mention he was fine. David was tall,slim, lightskin and he had green eyes. He resembles *Boris Kojoe*. I liked everything about him and the fact that he was different from the boys I went to school with. He said he was eighteen but that didn't matter to me, he was making me feel good and I was starting to fall for him.

We finally took our conversations from the phone and he asked if he could pick me up from school one day. I happily accepted his offer. The next day he scooped me up from school and I brought Shermaine along. He took us over to his homeboy house. The house wasn't in the best neighborhood but as long as I was with David I didn't care. We walked into the house and it was unkept, wasn't dirty but there were things all over the place which made it hard to get comfortable.

He introduced Shermaine and I to his homeboy Eric and I could already tell Eric was going to try to get with Shermaine by the way he was looking at her. Shermaine was boy crazy like I was but she had a thing for older men. The older the better was her motto.

Shermaine was already having sex with older men and in return they bought her whatever she couldn't get from her mother. Their money helped her buy the designer stuff she always dreamed of wearing. Eric started flirting with Shermaine and she entertained him because of me. I found myself a seat on the couch.

David walks into the kitchen and brings back a bottle of liquor and a couple of red cups. He takes up the seat next to me and put the bottle of liquor on the coffee table right next to some cigars and a bag of weed. He pours the liquor into the cups and hands me one and then he proceeds to roll up some weed.

Eric grabs two cups and hands one to Shermaine, they disappear into the back room. Eric was not Shermaine's type, he had no money. I was glad she was willing to take one for the team because I really wanted to be there with David. David lit the blunt and passes it to me but I declined.

I sipped on my drink and I could feel myself getting tipsy. David put the blunt down and started kissing me. His kisses were like honey, sweet. He was a good kisser better than anyone I've kissed before.

He laid me back on the couch and we continued kissing and then I felt his hands on my breast as he lifted my shirt and removed my bra and proceeded to have his way with them. Everything felt so good, he was so gentle. He then grabbed my hand and walked me to one of the bedrooms.

He sat down on the bed and pulled me onto his lap, he began to grind on me. It felt so good. He then flipped me over and he was back on top of me, kissing me on my lips, my breast and finally down my stomach. He pulled my pants off and I got nervous. I had never had sex before, but I knew I wanted it with him.

I whispered in his ear "this is my first time."

He looked me in my eyes and said, "I won't hurt you, I love you!"

I allowed him to follow through, although it was quite painful at first. I felt good to share my love with the man I loved and the man who loved me.

It's been about a year since David and I met and things between David and I moved quite fast. We were together almost every day. As I spent more time with David, I learned more and more about him. He was a nickel and dime drug dealer. He grew up rough, with no father and his mother struggled raising him in the projects. He desperately wanted a better life for himself and saw selling drugs as his way out.

David was very insecure, even though he was fine, he lacked confidence and always thought I was going to leave him to be with someone else, because he was out cheating on me. I constantly had to reassure him that I was down for him and he knew that to be sure when he got locked up for eight months and I was putting money on his books and going to visit him whenever I could. That was a rough few months without him, but I held him down and I kept myself for him.

When David was released out of jail, things resumed back to normal, I was about sixteen at the time and he was back in the streets nickel and diming and we were having sex like it was going out of style.

David was my man and I would have done anything for him, I was even more excited when I found out I was pregnant, and we were going to be a real family. I gave birth to our son Damian and we couldn't have been happier. David was the love of my life; he was the love I was looking for.

Chapter 3

Toxic Love

The years sped by and I had just celebrated my seventeenth birthday. I settled into my role as a mother of a one year old and as a faithful girlfriend. Motherhood brought me so much joy and brought a love I never knew I could feel. I was happy to have a family with David, he was the man I loved and he loved me. We found an apartment for our family and I was ready to finally be on my own with David and our son.

We were doing well on our own for a while, but the bills were piling up and David wasn't really making any money selling drugs, so I did what I knew best and I called on my parents to help us foot the bill.

Although they had their reservations about taking care of a grown man, they made it happen for me and Damian.

I thought David would have been appreciative towards my parents for all their help, but it made him cold and resentful towards me. He claimed I was stripping him of his manhood. I had to make a way, I've seen my mother do it and now that I was a mother I refused to struggle and to have my family out on the street. After school and on the weekends,I started keeping some of the children in the apartment complex just to bring in a little money. That pissed David off even more.

The tension grew between us and what was once a fairytale love became toxic and we started to destroy one another. David started staying out late,he was still seeing other women and he started blowing his money doing whatever he wanted. We fought, we argued and with each passing day his love towards me felt like hate.

Everything fell on me, not only was I arguing and fighting with his other women, I was paying all the bills, going to school and still giving him sex on the regular. He started questioning me about my whereabouts every time I left the house.

I couldn't even go school or to get groceries without him wanting to smell my vagina when I returned home. He became insecure and jealous about me leaving the house because he knew he was out screwing any and everything when he walked out those doors.

I remember this one Friday night, his jealousy rose to another level. I was finally getting a break from my normal routine. Shermaine invited me out to a local lounge. I was so excited to go, it had been a while since I did anything for myself and by myself, I jumped at the offer. My mother agreed to keep Damian. I was ready for some fun. I missed Shermaine, I hadn't seen her in a while because I was so focused on David and the baby.

We talked on the phone occasionally to one another, she was aware of the drama I've been living in. She began to dislike David every time I would tell her about his indiscretions.

She wanted me to let him go but I couldn't, he was my family. David was already out doing his thing, so I was able to get dressed in peace. I wanted to look pretty because I haven't felt pretty in a long time. It was the middle of July and the weather was still hot, so I decided to put on my short Tommy Hilfiger denim skirt. I paired it with a with a short sleeve white blouse and tan open toe sandals. I took off my scarf and unwrapped my hair and it fell past my shoulders. I sprayed a little oil sheen to give it a shine. I finished the outfit with three gold necklaces and my small gold hoops. I looked in the mirror and shockingly I looked good, but I also felt good. Shermaine came to pick me up. I jumped in the car and we sped down the street as *"Hypnotize" by Notorious BIG* came blasting through the speakers.

We arrived at the lounge and it was nice, and small, but there was a nice crowd of people inside. Shermaine walked us over to a table where an older gentleman who kind of resembled *Denzel Washington* was sitting. When he noticed us approaching, he stood up to embrace Shermaine and then he gave me a hug.

"Michael, this is my girl Lauren."

"Hi,Lauren, nice to meet you, you're beautiful."
He said in a deep baritone voice.

"Thank you, nice to meet you too." I said
blushing.

Michael offered to buy us drinks and quickly
left to go to the bar. Shermaine gave me the
scoop about him.

He was forty-two, she met him at the
Mall. She said he has a lot of money and loves
spending it on her. Their relationship wasn't
official, but they were exclusive to one another.
We shared a few more stories and he came back
with our drinks. He kissed Shermaine and then
he disappeared into the crowd.

"Where's he goin'?" I asked.

"Girl,he just came to give me some money."
She said with a smirk on her face.

I loved seeing her happy but I was
secretly jealous wishing David was that type of
man.She grabbed my hand and pulled me on
the dance floor and we danced the night away.
Men were coming up to us left and right.

Some even tried to get my number but I declined because of my loyalty to David. The crowd began to dissipate and Shermaine and I decided to leave.

Before dropping me off Shermaine wanted to stop at the corner store to get something to drink. I told her to make it quick because I had to beat David home. She ran inside the store, next thing I know David walks out of the store. Out of all nights, why did I have to run into him this night. My stomach dropped; I was nervous. David looks towards Shermaine's car, we lock eyes and he walks over to the car and opens the car door.

"Yo, what the fuck you doin out here?" he questioned angrily.

"I just went to a lounge with Shermaine, she wanted to get me out of the house."

"Why, so she can hook you up with other niggas, that bitch dirty, she know you got a man."

"D, it wasn't even like that, we went and had a good time, she won't hookin' me up with no niggas."

He grabbed me by my arm and pulled me out of the car.

"Nothing happened, you trippin over nothin."

"What the fuck ever, this bitch took you to a lounge because she trying to get you to cheat on me, I ain't stupid, this bitch, don't want you with me."

"D, ain't nobody cheatin on you!" I screamed.

"Get the fuck in the car, we goin home." He demanded.

"I gotta wait for Shermaine."

"Man fuck that bitch, get in the fuckin car!"

"Can I just tell her I'm leavin' with you."

"Fuck that, I'll tell that bitch!"

Shermaine finally came out of the store and as she was getting in her car. David yelled out his window.

"You dirty bitch, tryna get my bitch to cheat on me,fuck you, she leavin with me!" and he spun down the street.

We argued the entire drive home. We tussled a bit in the car, he stuck his finger inside my vagina, trying to figure out if I cheated on him. He was proved wrong but that didn't stop him from cursing me out and calling me all types of names. When we got inside the apartment, he pushed me onto the couch, pulled his penis out and penetrated me.

"This pussy is mine, and if I ever find out you givin it away to other niggas. I will fuck you up."

After that night, David's behavior didn't get better and to ease his mind, I tried to limit the times I left the house. I called to apologize to Shermaine and thankfully she accepted my apology and our friendship was still intact.

No matter what he did, I held on tighter. I don't know if it was because I was missing my father's love or what, but I couldn't shake him.

Over these past few months, my dad grew distant, he stopped coming around and our phone conversations became non-existent. David was giving me the loved I thought I needed. In the mist of everything, I was still trying to be a good girlfriend to a man who mistreated and abused me.

David first put his hands on me when he came home, and I was packing up some clothes for me and the baby. It was the summer after my eighteenth birthday. I had just graduated from high school and I was preparing to leave him. I had enough, I grew tired of him cheating on me. I was tired of him not having any money and I was tired of him treating me like trash when I was the only one holding him down. We exchanged a few nasty words as I continued packing up my things.

He came over and pushed me on the bed and told me I wasn't going anywhere. I tried to get up, but he climbed on top of me pinning me down on the bed. I started yelling and trying to fight back but he was too strong, the more I fought, the tighter he gripped my hands pushing all his weight on me.

I screamed, he loosened his grip and took that same hand and slapped me cold across the face. A single tear seeped from my eyes. I couldn't believe the man I loved just hit me. I couldn't believe this was my life. I just laid there, shocked, confused and afraid. Then, I felt his lips press against mine and the next words out of his mouth was

"I'm Sorry." He climbed off me and start apologizing. "I didn't mean to hit you, I'm sorry, I just don't want you to leave me, I need you and baby D. I need my family. I promise if you stay, I'll never do it again, I'll never cheat again. I'll never hurt you Lauren." David pleaded as the tears swelled up in his eyes.

I've never seen David this way, I had never seen him cry, my anger and fear turned into compassion as I watched a man show remorse for his actions. I naively believed him, I believed he truly wanted me and his family, I believed his loved for me was real because he only hit me because he didn't want me to leave. I began to make excuses for David because of love, and I allowed David to use "love" to keep me tied to him.

■■

There I was again, applying ice to my black eye, the black eye, I receive from a man who claimed he loved me. The promises David made was short-lived as the abuse continued for eight years. At twenty-six years old I continued to take David's abuse.

"Love" was the reason I stayed. I loved David and even though he put me through so much, I still believed he "loved" me because he kept coming home to me.

He kept choosing me. David was in the same position he was in all those years ago, broke and still cheating. I carried the weight for the entire family, David became my second child.I thought I could show David a better way, I thought I could show him real love. I thought I could change him but he wasn't ready to do better.

David was going to do whatever he wanted, and the family suffered from it all. I didn't tell a soul. I tried to hide the abuse from my family, but my mother knew and she begged me on several occasions to leave him.

I would give her the same answer "I love him, and I want my family, he's getting better." I continued to make excuses for David and his behavior and everyone around me knew. This was the only love I knew, and it was the love I decided to keep even when it kept growing toxic.

In the mist of our dysfunction, I found myself pregnant again. I gave birth to our daughter Destiny and for the first time in a long time, I was happy. It was nice to see David bond with our baby girl. When Destiny was about one month old, I finally had enough, I was tired of the cheating and him beating on me.

I gave David an ultimatum. I told David if he didn't stop beating me, if he didn't stop nickeling and diming, if he didn't stop cheating, I was going to leave him for good. I was serious. I don't know what snapped within him, but he took my threats serious.

He stepped up for the family in a major way. He stopped cheating and was spending every night at home. He started making more money. When he would come home, I would take some of the money and stash it away. In one month, I saved about twenty thousand dollars.

He was surprised that I could save so much in such a short time. I had to remind him of who I was. I showed him how to open a legit bank account and to flip his money and do a legit business. From the money we saved, we bought a few cars to flip and we began to live a little better.

David wasn't into taking handouts, he wanted to be the man for his family. He informed me that he wanted to make more money for the family. I decided to turn him on to a new connect, my brother Paul. Paul convinced me to bring in David and Paul showed him how to go from moving dimes to keys.

Things were looking up for us and after few months of good living, he decided to propose to me. This felt right, I accepted his proposal and we were married shortly after. The money came in quickly, we began to live the life I always dreamed. We bought us a big house, a house you'll see up in the Hollywood Hills. We drove the best cars and we were on the party scene. I opened a small childcare center. We turned into a Power couple overnight.

Life was finally going good until that one fall night we received a knock on the door, and it was the Police, arresting my husband for murder.

Chapter 4

A Mother's Love

After David was cleared of his charges, he got a boost of confidence and began to think he was untouchable. He was doing right for about four years. We did it up for one another and our children. They received the best of the best for their birthdays, for Christmas and random times when they asked. We took lavish trips, ate at the best restaurants. If they didn't know anything, they knew we loved them. They had every material possession a person could ever want.

The good living proved too be too much for David as he was slowly falling back into old habits.

He became "The Man" in his own eyes and people was blowing up his head, he reverted to his old ways of blowing money on cocaine and sleeping with strippers.

I was exhausted trying to run a business, trying to be a wife to him and trying to be a mother to him and our children. If it wasn't for me securing the Lawyer, posting the bail, he'll still be sitting in jail for a crime he didn't commit. Then he repays me by disrespecting me and neglecting our family. I decided I was done and separated from my husband.

Our separation took a toll on the children and Damian began to act out. Damian was a preteen and he desperately needed his father. He was losing focus in school and I can't tell you how many times I've been called to the school for his poor behavior. Even though he was acting out, I couldn't help but shower him and his sister with whatever they wanted to compensate for their dad's behavior. They were my children, I wanted them to have everything their heart desires, after all isn't that how a mother loves her children.

It was the beginning of the new school year in 2006, Damian was twelve years old.

The year hadn't fully started, and I received a call from the school informing me that Damian was in a fight.

I jumped in the car and rushed to the school, the entire drive there, I was blowing David's phone up because his son needed him, but I never got a response.

Typical David, not there for us when it mattered. Damian received five days suspension for fighting someone for talking about his dad and there I was taking him through the drive-thru to get his favorite food because he was hungry, and I was trying to cover up why David couldn't be there. I know I should have made him eat whatever we had at home, but I know he's only acting out because of David so why should I punish him because of his daddy's lack of attention.

We talked and he agreed he wouldn't fight again, and he'll learned how to control his temper. I was pissed that I was doing this all on my own, they had a father, but I had to pick up his slack while he entertained hoes. I continued to give them a good life the best way I knew how, I still hoped that David would eventually do right and come back to his family.

I settled into life as a "separated woman" and I was doing ok. It wasn't necessary what I wanted for my family, but it was needed to get away from David until he got himself together. My childcare center was doing well, and I was in the process of opening another one.

I heard through the grapevine that David got an apartment and come to find out he came back to the home we had together and went through the safe and took all my money to pay for it. I was furious, I couldn't believe this man would take from me and from his children. I remember going over my mother's house, tears running down my cheeks and I just laid in her lap. I was exhausted, I just wanted to be free from the drama. Free from this man.

David forgot about me and the children. He stripped us of his love. At twenty-eight years old as I laid in my mother's lap, I realized I still needed her love. I told her everything that was going on between David and me. I knew she had my gun stashed away in her closet, I told her to keep that one just in case I needed it, and this was that time.

"Ma, go in your closet and get my gun." I demanded.

"Lauren, why you need your gun, don't do nothing crazy,David ain't worth it."

"I ain't going to do nothin to David, I'm just going to talk, and I need some protection." I lied.

She left to go and grab my gun.

"Lauren, think about the children, he aint worth it." She tried to reason with me as she hands me the gun.

"I got it under control Ma, this is for protection." I said as I kissed her on the cheek.

I put the gun in my purse, I grabbed Destiny and I hopped in my car determined to teach David a lesson. On the ride over there, I thought of so many ways I could shoot him and claim self-defense. I was informed on the gun laws so I knew that could work in my favor. I was nervous, I called my brother Paul.

"Hello." He said into the receiver.

"Paul!" I said hysterically. "I know I shouldn't do what I'm about to do but just make sure you have money to bail me out of jail and please take care of my children if I can't make bail."

Paul didn't ask any questions, all he said was "As long as it isn't over a million dollars."

We exchanged "I love you's" and I hung up the phone.

I made it to David's apartment, my heart was pounding, and my mind was racing with a million thoughts per minute. I couldn't believe I was here to kill my husband and the father of my two children, but I was done. He stole my money, the money I was using to take care of his two children. It wasn't like he was helping me at the time. He took our money and moved into an apartment to shack up with some nasty white bitch.

Then, he had people running around town trashing me talking about how would I make it without him. They had the nerve to imply that "I wasn't with him shooting in the gym".

He won't no damn Kobe anyway. They forgot it was me that helped build that motherfucking gym, I was with him when he was shooting in the gym, when he had nothing. I taught David how to get money. Everything he has was because of me. The question should have been how he will survive without me. I was ready and it was time he meets his maker.

My thoughts were interrupted when Destiny started whining about food. She kept saying she was hungry. It was her voice that brought me back to reality. I had every intent to kill this man, but my beautiful daughter stopped it. When I turned and looked at her, I knew I couldn't be away from her, she needed me. I couldn't let her lose that even if her dad wasn't acting right. I put the car into reverse and backed out of the parking lot. I had children who needed me.

A few months after showing up to David's apartment, he started coming around, spending time with the children. They were glad to have their dad back in their lives. He tried to get back with me, but I couldn't jump back into things with him.Even though he was there for the children, I was still in a bad space with him, I was still hurt and broken.

I thought we were going to be in this thing forever. I realized David couldn't give me the love I wanted because he didn't have the capacity to love me, he didn't even love himself. Hell, I didn't even love myself. We both only knew toxic love, but that kind of love wasn't good anymore, our children deserved to see their parents love one another where that love produced smiles and not constant tears and dysfunction. I decided to file papers to divorce David.

David wasn't happy about me filing the divorce papers, he refused to sign them giving me the run around for months. Although I proceeded with the divorce, I cried when I filed the paperwork with the courts. It hurt me as well, but I knew this was best. I wanted us to move forward with our lives and learn how to co-parent, so Damian and Destiny knew that we both loved them. As soon as David started to become the father he wanted to be and the children needed, his past pulled him away from them.

David was arrested, the feds picked him up on drug charges. It was Destiny's birthday and he came over to the house to drop some money off for her party and the feds followed him to the house. I remember Damian running upstairs yelling.

"ma, ma, daddy outside with the police."

I rushed downstairs confused and discombobulated. Damian brushed passed me and ran to his daddy. He started pulling on him asking the police to let him go.
The police then drew their guns on my child. I began yelling.

"Stop, ya'll he is just a child crying for his daddy, ya'll could put ya'll guns away, he ain't doing nothing wrong. That's his damn daddy!"

They withdrew their guns. Destiny runs out of out the house crying with a bible in hand, telling her daddy God loves him. She tries to give the bible to her dad, but the police wouldn't allow her to. We all locked eyes and it was in that moment I knew their lives would forever be changed. All of us were in tears. We all shared a hug and they ripped us apart and put David in the back of the police car.
When the police drove out of our driveway, both of my children hit the pavement. They were crying hysterically.

After about twenty minutes of them crying, I was able to get them inside the house. I called my mother and she came over to comfort the children and me. I felt bad for him and for our children. I know there are consequences in life, but it hurt to see a man I once was in love with, and the father of my children be stripped away from them.

I had to put my feelings for David aside and I had to be there for our children because their life was changing in more ways than we could have ever imagined.

****

It's been about four and half years since David got locked up, they found him guilty of the crime and he wasn't going to be getting released any time soon and according to my lawyer that was the best time to finalize our divorce .

On one hand I was glad to be free from David, and on the other hand his absence took a toll on the children and surprisingly on me. They missed him so much, I did my best to make their life seem as normal as possible.

I made sure they wanted for nothing hoping those material things could make them feel better.

Even though Damian was hanging with the wrong people and getting into trouble at school. I still stuck with my mother's tradition and bought him a foreign car for his sixteenth birthday. I wanted him to have the best, no matter how he behaved at school or at home. Looking back, I realized he wasn't quite ready for that type of responsibility and I should not have gave into him.

Things took a turn for the worst when Damian called me from jail. Damian was arrested for riding in a stolen car with his friends, they also found guns inside the car. This boy had everything, I gave him everything his mind could want, he had the good life and yet he still found his way into trouble.

I was livid but I needed my son home with me. His bond was 130,000 and like any mother, I posted it to get my son home. I couldn't see him sitting in jail like his father. I did for my son the same thing I did for his father; I acquired the best lawyer money could buy and I was determined to have Damian cleared of all charges.

Damian convinced me that he didn't know anything about the guns or the stolen car and as crazy as it sounded, I believed him.

He must have had a special place in God's heart because one of his friends confessed and told police that Damian had nothing to do with stealing the car.
The detective called us down to the station and they dismissed the charges. I couldn't do nothing but fall on my knees and thank the Lord. I needed to get Damian a mentor or a father figure to help keep him on the right track. He needed a male role model my love could only go so far.

Paul convinced me to let him be active in Damian's life. Although we had our disagreements in the past, he claimed he would make it up to me by being there for Damian since his father was in the feds. I knew Paul wasn't squeaky clean, but he promised me that he wouldn't involve Damian in any parts of that lifestyle, and I believed him.

When Damian found out he would be spending more time with Paul he was so excited. He looked up to him, and in Damian's mind his uncle was a real O.G.

Damian loved the type of life he lived. He saw Paul as a boss, a man that owns businesses and a man that lives a good life. Damian loved his Uncle Paul.

Over the next two years Paul and Damian grew closer. Damian was doing better in school and he graduated with a 3.2 GPA and was doing better around the house and I was grateful for Paul for stepping in as a father to help my son.

After high school he decided he didn't want to go to college, he showed interest in opening his own used car business like his dad. He said his Uncle Paul showed him how much money he could make in week from selling and flipping cars. Paul later came to me and asked me to invest in the business for Damian. I was a little iffy at first because of past business dealings with Paul but Damian was doing well and seemed very excited about this. I willing to do anything for Damian, to see him become successful.

My mother and I got together with Paul, and we bought a few used cars from the auction for him to flip. I paid for him to take a few classes, so he could learn the ins and outs of credit, loans and selling cars.

The business started off slow, but it was quickly moving in the right direction.

I was so proud of Damian for turning his life around and I hoped this business would help him stay focused and on the right path but boy was I wrong, it was this exact business that put my son in a position to take a charge for his Uncle Paul.

I later found out that Paul was running an illegal operation through Damian's Car shop. When the police busted in my mom and son were inside the shop and they arrested them both.

The Feds harassed my son, they pulled out every tactic they could to get him to talk, they were trying to get him to give up his uncle Paul. They even took Damian's car thinking that would get them what they wanted but Damian stayed strong and didn't break. He did say it was all on him so that my mother could walk away because they were trying to charge her. She didn't want Damian to go down by himself so she confessed to a much lesser charge, which later on she just had to pay restitution for, but Damian was facing felony charges.

When Damian needed Paul the most, he turned his back on him and I had to rescue my son. Paul never came to the jail, he never called to see if my son was ok.

My son gave up his life for his uncle so I'll never understand why he would leave his own nephew high and dry without as much as an apology and a thank you.

There I was pulling money from the childcare center's account to cover his bail of 260,000. When my son was finally released into my custody, he confessed that he took the charge because he didn't want to see another man, he loved go to jail.

Paul was all he had since his dad been away and his relationship with my dad was nonexistent. He felt it was on him to keep the only father figure he knew out of prison.

He asked to call Paul and I had to let him know Paul shitted on him and it was Paul that set him up. I informed him that he was going to have to face these charges alone but that I was going to lawyer up to see that he remained a free man.

This situation took a toll of all of us. I had to cut my only brother off and now I had to deal with the fact that if our lawyer couldn't do his job, my son would be spending all his youth behind bars.

We spent about six months on pins and needles and God shined down on Damian once again and his charges was dropped to misdemeanors. He was put on probation, he had to do community service and pay a few fines. I told Damian he better give thanks to God for everything he has done to keep his black ass out of jail. I had conversations with him over the years but that day I wanted to drill into his head that the streets don't love him, that type of life isn't meant for him because if anything was to happen to him, it will hurt me and the family.

I also reminded him that not every friend will be there for him when things get tough and he needs to make sure he chooses his friends wisely. He listened to me without any interruptions so I'm sure he was digesting my words.

After everything Damian had been through over these past few years, he was able to get himself together, I helped him open a t-shirt business.

He was on his way towards success and the blessing behind it all, he was able to get his record expunged. He was truly a free man.

The night after I received news that Damian's record was expunged, I walked into my bathroom to shower hoping to wash the day away when I noticed my reflection in the mirror the tears began to gush out. I had been dealing with so much and I was worn out. I couldn't help but see my mother, I was becoming her. I was loving my children the way she loved me and my brother.

She took that charge for Paul so he wouldn't go to prison, he was facing federal time of about twenty plus years. She used her credit to buy things for Paul's first home. She took care of his wife, treated her like her own daughter. My mother took up for her when Paul was cheating with other women and now his wife won't even speak to my mom but let something go down and she's the first one they call to clean up their mess.

She co-signed on a motorcycle for Paul. She would do anything for that boy, that's the way she loved. If he asked, she gave and there I was doing the same thing for Damian. I gave him everything he could ever want.

I bailed him out of trouble more times than I could count. I sacrificed the profits from my two businesses, sometimes going in the red for him and his sister. I wanted them to know how much I loved them but maybe I loved them in a way that will cripple them for life.

Chapter 5

Family Love

Family was always important to me, that is why I stayed with David for so long. Having people, you could count on in the time of trouble, people who would love you unconditionally was all I ever wanted. My family means the world to me, so I was devastated when I had to cut my own brother off. I loved Paul, we were always close growing up.

Those summers with Paul and Daddy were always the best. Even though Paul was a boy and I was a girl, anything he was a part of I wanted to be a part of too.

We played basketball together, we played with his action figures and we loved playing tag.

We were two peas in the pod. I remember when Daddy took us for ice cream and Paul ordered five scoops of chocolate chip ice cream and I ordered the same, Daddy knew I wouldn't eat that much but because Paul had it, I had to have it too. I ended up wasting half of it. I was his shadow, and I just couldn't believe how selfish he became as we got older.

I was always a hustler, I got that mentality from my mother but if I ever needed something I couldn't get, Paul was there for me. There was no question that Paul had my back because I had his, that's what family did. When Paul went out on a limb to put David on, I believed Paul was looking out for the family. I thought he wanted us all to eat but something changed with Paul, I don't know if it was the money or what it was, but Paul let whatever it was get the best of him and caused him to hurt his own flesh and blood.

The problems between Paul and me hurt our mother dearly. We were her only children and it hurt her to see that I wasn't speaking to my brother and it hurt her to see the person Paul became.

She tried to get us back talking, trying to put us on three way but every time I heard his voice, I would hang up. I let my mother know I needed time and I just didn't know if I want to have a relationship with Paul. My mother out of all people should understand where I'm coming from because she has also suffered because of Paul's selfishness.

Back in 2008, Paul approached my mother and me about a business opportunity that he wanted us to invest in. My mother and I invested quite a lot of money into his "business opportunity". We helped him get the business up and running and me and my mother ended up doing a lot of the foot work for the business for free because he had no one.

We were even passing flyers out in the rain. The business ended up turning a profit and he sold the business for half a million. Paul took all the money for himself, he didn't even give a dime to me or my mother but when the business started failing, there was Paul calling my mother or me to help him out.

Now that I look back Paul likes to use people for his benefit and whenever he's done with them, he disposes them. Money made Paul a different man.

That situation left a bad taste in my mouth when it came to Paul but he was my brother, so I forgave him and my children loved him and I wanted them to have their uncle in their life, that's why I wanted him to mentor Damian. I wish I would've just cut ties with him after the business situation and my son would've never been caught up in his illegal bullshit, but you live, and you learn. I learned that when a person shows you who they are, believe them even if they are family.

Paul knew he had my mother wrapped around his finger though, she was always at his beck and call, she bailed him out more times than I could count. I loved my mother and over the years we have grown extremely close, she was my best friend, but I didn't like how she was with Paul. I just wish she would put her foot down and let him fend for himself, but I guess as I went through those same things with my son, I could see why she just wouldn't let him learn the hard way.

My mother was always trying to make sure everyone was good, that's what I loved most about her, that she was a giver. She loved her children and her grandchildren are her world. She spent a lot of time with them, keeping them when I was in school and she would also pick them up a couple weekends out of each month to take them to do something fun. My mother also helped me behind the scenes with my childcare centers.

She was there for us whenever I would call. Her support kept me going over the years. As I got older, we became closer, we took trips together and I showered her with love. Our Favorite Trip was down to Atlanta, I took her to *Gladys Knights Chicken and Waffles*. We ate and enjoyed ourselves. I wish I had that same bond with my father.

My dad and I started drifting apart in my twenties, he became busy with his own life. It was Paul who walked me down the aisle when my dad had an excuse on why he couldn't make it to the wedding but had the nerve to ask if we could send him a plate. I reached out to him frequently and my calls would go unanswered.

I finally got tired of being the only one to reach out, so I stopped. He even grew apart from his grandchildren. My children don't know him at all. I wanted them to know the fun parts of him, the parts of him I remembered from the summers I spent with him and from the times he would pick me up and hug me.

I would give anything to have that bond with him again, but things have just gone too far.

My dad remarried and that hurt me to see that he had time for his wife and her family but not for me and my children. He even had time for Paul, they would hang every so often. I wish I knew what kept him away from me and for years I tried to figure out why he took his love away, but I never received that answer. I saw a lot of my dad in Paul and it hurt that the two men I loved dearly would hurt me the way they have.

They were both selfish and only thought of self and didn't care how their actions affected me. From how things are looking now I didn't know if my family would ever get it right.

Chapter 6

A Journey to Self-Love

From the outside looking in, it looked as if I had it made, my children were doing well and living their lives and my childcare centers were still bringing in excellent profits. I kept myself up physically but deep inside I was struggling trying to find my way. I was going through it with my brother and I still didn't have a relationship with my father. I wasn't living the life I knew I could live. I was just existing going with the motions.

Over the past 20 years or so, since I was fourteen, I poured myself into everyone I loved, every piece of me they received, but I never gave myself any love.

I was last on my list and I allowed myself to be mistreated and disrespected by a man who said he loved me.

I've thought about David on occasions and there were times I missed him and craved his touch but then I quickly remembered the bullshit he put me through and I knew I needed real love, I wanted to be loved the right way. After the dust settled with Damian's situation, I wanted to start doing things for me, I missed hanging with my girls, I missed the company of a man, I missed traveling. I missed me and I was determined to find myself so I could give her the love she lacked over the past years.

It was 2014 and over the next few months I was on a journey of getting back to Lauren and life was going well. I was spending more time with my girls and in a few weeks, we were going to meet each other in New Orleans for a girl's trip.I missed Shermaine so much over the years. We stayed in touch via the telephone and on social media, but I didn't see her as much because she hated David and he felt the same. Shermaine herself had a rough couple of years as she found herself stripping down in Atlanta.

She said it was slow at first but once she found her groove. She began to bring in the dough. Shermaine was the epitome of a chocolate Barbie doll and her body was everything. The older she got the more she reminded you of Gabrielle Union or JuJu, the rapper CamRon's ex-girlfriend. She would often rave about how the men down in Atlanta couldn't get enough of her. Over the years she stayed with a Sugar Daddy and later fell in love with one who gave her the world. She ended up pregnant, she decided to stop stripping her Sugar Daddy who was now her husband moved her back up to North Carolina. Shermaine seemed to be happy, so I couldn't wait to catch up with her down in New Orleans.

My bags were packed, and I was on my way to New Orleans, it felt good to be living life for myself and I was on my way to loving Lauren again. Shermaine and I decided to catch the same flight and it was like old times when we reconnected at the terminal. Once we arrived in New Orleans, we waited at the airport for my girl Trice. Trice was older than me she was about forty-six.

She was a hard worker and an attorney at a Prestigious Law Firm in Raleigh, North Carolina. She's one of the grandparents to a child at my childcare center who I've had since they were an infant.

Trice invited me to an event her job was having, and we had a blast and we clicked, and she's been my girl ever since. Trice is a beautiful girl, light beautiful skin, she wears her hair short like *Halle Berry in "Boomerang"* she's what they consider a BBW but she carries it well. She's appears confident but she's very insecure about her weight. Trice is the opposite of Shermaine, she is bossy, and she loves to control and take care of men.

She's the Sugar Momma to these young men. Trice would do anything to keep those young boys happy. Threesomes, wild sex, whatever they wanted, Trice was down to give it to them but this current man Ahmad, was giving her a run for her money but you couldn't tell Trice nothing, she was the type of person that would ask for advice and do the opposite. Trice finally arrived, and we shared a hug. I introduced the girls to one another; we grabbed a taxi and we made our way over to our hotel. We got settled into our rooms, rested for a bit and then we got dressed for dinner.

"Ladies, this way to your table." The young hostess said as she led us to our table.

We placed our orders for our drinks and the conversation flowed.

I missed ya'll, this trip was so needed." I said.

"I know girl, after everything with Damian, this is what you needed." Shermaine said. "How are the kids doing?"

"Girl, Damian is doing better, he took those charges like a man, he's been focused and on the right track and I don't think he's going to be getting into any more trouble. He has his business and after the whole ordeal, he rather make money but that shit took a lot out of me and the family. That year was rough, trying to be there for Damian and Destiny.
I felt like I was been pulled in so many directions, but I had to do what I had to do, that was my damn son and he wasn't going to be locked in no damn cage and then Destiny used to cry a lot over her damn daddy, she even wrote the president and shit trying to see if he could bring her daddy home.

Lately I've been trying to give her extra love and spend more time with her to keep her busy and her mind off of it and then when Damian was in that same situation, she felt like she was losing another father figure. She's so sweet though, she's cheerleading and so smart in school."

"Lauren girl, I admire that about you,you be dealing with a lot shit but you still keep your head up." Trice said.

"Yea, but behind closed doors, them tears be falling, sometimes I get tired of everything. Paul that got him caught up in that bullshit, but in front of those cops it was death before dishonor, he remained loyal, never folding. I believe that's why Paul did everything he did because he knew my son would never rat him out. I still can't believe it was my motherfuckin' brother that set my damn son up. That was so fuckin' hard to hear,and I had to stop fuckin' with him. We were like two peas in the pod but that nigga ain't been the same since we were younger. It's just fucked up because you think you could always count on family because it's automatic love but sometimes blood just ain't that thick."

"Damn, Paul did that shit, I remember when we use to spend those summers with your dad, who would ever think Paul would do some bullshit like that." Shermaine said.

"I still can't believe it, my own flesh and blood, the brother I share the same father and mother with would turn his back on us and leave his own family out to dry. What's sad is Damian was going to protect him to the end, he loved Paul like a father, it's sad that Paul didn't love him like a son. I don't even know how I'm going to move past this, I'm fucking pissed at Paul and if I ever saw him again, I don't know what I would do. Then my own dad was talking trash about Damian. My mom told my dad that Damian couldn't open a bank account because the feds will take his money and my dad was like "oh well he don't have money like Paul so it don't matter. " My dad put all the blame on Damian and acted like Paul didn't do a thing. He acted like my son was the problem. That shit hurt, especially from family. The only person I could truly count on is my mother, because my dad and my brother only care about themselves and I finally get it now, I will never let Paul burn me or my children again."

"Just know that we love you girl forreal and you don't have to worry about that bullshit with us, we got your back forreal." Trice said and she stood up to hug me.

"Yea we got you girl, it's all love over here, we're sisters forever." Shermaine added as she touched my hand.

I wiped the tears from my eyes and decided it was time to switch up the mood, we were supposed to be having a ball and I didn't want to bring down the mood with my sad stories.

"Sooo, Trice, what's been up with you and your man?" I asked.

"Ahmad been getting on my nerves, doing stupid shit." Trice said rolling her eyes. "What he do this time?" I inquired giving her the side eye.

"What is he not doing!" Trice said laughing. "I give this little boy everything he could ever want, good sex, good head, I just bought him some jays and I gave him money to get a game for his little Playstation. A few weeks ago, he was at my house and he was acting strange, real strange taking his phone everywhere he went as if I wasn't going to see the type of bullshit, he on. So, I fucked him good y'all, laid his little young ass out because a girl had to get into that nigga phone. He is so damn stupid his password was basic as hell. So, I go through his phone, go straight for the text messages, it's only like three threads, mines, his mother and his homeboy John. When he do shit like this I know he talking to other hoes, so I go to his Instagram account and BOOM, I hit the lottery. This fuck nigga, all in other bitches DM's tryna get them to fuck. Some took the bait and he actually met up with some of them bitches. I woke him up with a 3-piece combo to the dome. I give him everything and he thanks me by fucking other hoes."

"Damn that's fucked up, but you know he be doing bullshit, this isn't the first time Trice." I said.

"Yea, but his ass said he was going to do right, like he's stressing me the hell out, I can't even focus on making Partner at work because all of my energy and all of my time is spent on trying to get him to be faithful. Then the women he cheats on looks nothing like me, all those hoes skinny or bodies be right, it be making me feel like he only with me for one thing."

"If I could leave David you could leave him alone, and you know how much I loved me some David."

"You loved that nigga hard girl." Shermaine said laughing. "You were gonna ride for that nigga no matter what."

"But I've been learning I deserve more, I thought David's love was all I could get but as I started healing, I realized love isn't abuse and having other bitches on the side."

"yea, you right." Trice agreed.

Trice agreed but I knew she wasn't going to leave Ahmad alone, there was something this young boy was giving her that had her hooked like glue.
I wanted better for her, but I can't force her to leave him, she'll have to do that when she gets ready.

The waiter placed our food down in front of us, Shermaine took a couple bites of food and she began to open up about her situation.

"You remember how much I hated David for the bullshit he was doing to you but I'm kinda in that same boat girl. You know when Chris and I first got together, everything was perfect. He showered me with gifts, and he made sure I had everything I needed. I loved him for that. After dealing with bullshit from men over the years I finally thought I lucked up until the phone calls started coming in."

Tears began to fall from her eyes.

"One call after another from a bitch telling me my man got her pregnant. This nigga damn near sixty and he had three women pregnant at the same damn time. Our daughter had just turned two and this bastard was sowing his seed all over Greensboro. I'm so damn tired ya'll, if I stay I gotta accept all these damn babies. I haven't decided what to do. Chris gives me a good fucking life, I don't want for nothing but damn does every nigga cheat, cause if so then I'll take my chances with Chris."

"Damn, that's fucked up." Trice added. "These niggas aint about shit, we love them hard and they shit on us in every way. Where are the good fucking men at!"

We share a laugh.

"Since we are sharing stories, let me tell ya'll about these two men I was talking to over the past couple of months., so I met this man and things was good initially. He wasn't that cute ya'll but he was nice so I continued to hang with him.He was a down to earth man, he had a little money.
We went out to eat a couple of times and went to a couple of events, he invited me to go down to Charlotte with him. I go and everything was cool, we partied, we went to waffle house but when we got back to the hotel. He came to my room and everything.
I faked a headache real quick, sent him to get me some Goody Powder and when he brought it back, I fake took it and told him I'll call him in the morning and went to sleep on that ass."
I started laughing.

"Girl you crazy as hell." Shermaine said laughing.

"I know he was pissed." Trice added.

"Probably was but he was doing too much, just because we had a good time, that doesn't mean he deserves some ass. When I got home, I blocked his number with the quickness, but let me tell ya'll about this other dude. Ima call him "Taurus".Taurus a big Teddy Bear and I loved his Philly accent, he was the average Joe, wasn't too flashy. I met him at a gas station, and we exchanged numbers. We kicked it a couple of times until he wanted to confess that he was married but he wasn't happy. He talked about how bad his wife was and how she didn't care about him and all this other stuff. I stopped seeing him, but I still took his calls, I know I probably shouldn't have done that, but I gave him a shoulder to cry on and he was a good listener when I needed to vent about my problems. I started encouraging him to do nice things for his wife, that maybe she was overworked and needed his support. Ya'll I became this man's therapist.

The more we talked the more he started to confess his feelings for me but ya'll I couldn't help this man break up his family. If I'm honest I did like him a little bit, but I didn't want to be his side chick. We never slept together, which I'm happy we didn't do, he kissed me once on the cheek. If he didn't have his wife, maybe it could have become something but I couldn't do that, I had to block his number."

"What the fuck Lauren, thank God you turned that nigga down, you see what I'm going through with Chris. Don't ever get involved with somebody else's man." Shermaine said.

"Naw, I almost got caught up but I remembered how I felt when David had all those hoes and I never want to be the woman who help a man cheat, I guess I just enjoyed his conversations, but I'm off that. There was a couple of other men I kicked it with, and I had some fun with, but those niggas were either too clingy or too controlling. I almost found myself back in another David situation, with Trey, y'all remember me telling y'all about Trey."

"Yeah" they say in unison.

"I thought he was good tho." Trice said.

"Yea at first but it became too much so I had to let him go as soon as I could and to think I almost fell in love with that one. Thank God I didn't though. Ya'll I've been thinking about doing me for a while, like no dating, just doing me, healing and growing. I'm tired of meeting men who don't mean well. I want that real love, I want me a good man."

"We all want a good man; I just don't think they're out here." Trice said.

The waiter brought us our check. We paid and left the restaurant and made our way to a little club.

■■■

It's been a few months since my trip to New Orleans with my girls and I needed that trip with them, we laughed, cried and had so much fun. After hearing everything they were going through and knowing what I went through I knew this journey of finding myself needed to happen. We were all living and loving wrong and I was determined not to be living and loving that way ever again.

When I got back from New Orleans, I felt rejuvenated, and I wanted to give back to other women. I decided to start an organization to help assist domestic violence survivors. I was passing out flyers and I ran into this lady who just gravitated towards me. Her name was Ms. Sandra and when I handed her a flyer we began talking as if we were best friends. She was gem of wisdom and said she would help me with my business because she was well connected and knew how to start Non-Profit Organizations.

We exchanged numbers and she invited me to lunch. Lunch was great, this was the first time I've spoken to a woman who understood healthy love. She was vibrant and out-going. She was confident and sure of herself and it was evident that she loved herself. She talked about her husband who went on to be with the Lord. She talked about their love and how it was important for their foundation to be built upon God.

She told me love doesn't have to hurt but in order to realize that you must understand self-love and what love really is. She wanted me to know that there are good men in the world and to never let my past make me bitter but use my past as fuel to make me better. She gave me several books to read that will help me along this journey of self-love.

Sometimes I think about why I went through the things I did but maybe it was to get me to this place where I could help others. After having lunch with Ms. Sandra, I knew I deserved a love that doesn't hurt, that doesn't belittle and that doesn't tear me down. I knew I needed to show up for myself by not hurting myself or allowing others to hurt me.

I spent a lot of years loving wrong, so I was going to spend the next few years getting this love thing right.

Chapter 7

Making Peace

Over the next couple of months, I was still journeying towards self-love. I separated myself from anyone or anything that reminded me how I used to live. I continued to live for me. I enrolled in one of our local colleges to pursue business. I wanted to show my children that no matter what obstacles come their way, it's never too late to go to school. I was excited about where my life was going. I grew extremely close to Ms. Sandra. She was the kind of woman I could model myself after. She was confident in her relationships with others. Self-love seeped from her pores and I wanted that for myself.

I was doing things for myself, traveling with my girls, traveling with my children and dating but it wasn't until Ms. Sandra's Sorority Luncheon that opened my eyes on what it means to truly love yourself.

I knew about self-care; I knew about cutting people off who meant me harm, but they touched on going inward and doing the hard work to heal inner pain from the past and or present. The things they were speaking about sounded foreign, but I knew I needed to hear those things if I wanted to love myself better.

"Thank you so much for inviting me here, Ms. Sandra." I said as we prepared to leave the luncheon.

"You're welcome sweetheart. They do these luncheons every year, we just want to inspire women to live better and to love better. Women of all races spend so much time taking care of everyone else that they forget to take care of themselves and we want to teach them how to balance it all."

"That was me, since the age of fourteen I took care of other people and I was last on my list. I loved my ex-husband, I believed I loved him the right way. I took him back every time he would cheat, I took him back after he would beat me. I thought that's what love did. I loved him more than I loved myself. I gave this man everything and what's so sad is after he got locked up, I still felt sorry for him.

Ms.Sandra, I still loved him and even considered getting back with him for the children. What was I thinking, how stupid could I be to still feel sorry for that man."

"It's because you're human and you only loved from what you believed love was. Many people operate that way, there are plenty of men and women who think love is dysfunctional. They think the more bull crap they put up with the stronger their love is and it's because many people are emotionally unhealthy. You're not stupid, you just didn't understand what healthy love looked like."

"That's what I want, I want love, the type of love that makes me feel better, and the type of love that grows me. A love where I am free to be me, I don't want to be a man's mother or take his cheating. I want a man who honors and respects me, I want a man who loves me in action and words and keeps his word. If he says he loves me, I want him to mean it by the way he treats me. If I'm honest, I don't know if I'll ever get that man."

"You can, you just have to believe that's what you deserve but before you get that man, you have to become the woman you need to be, you need to spend time getting healthy. I believe that you'll have the life you need, continue to take time for yourself and learn what healthy love look like, I have some books at the house, and I'll bring them for you to read they will help you in this journey."

Tears fell from my eyes. I was so grateful for her, I've seen a lot of things in this life, but she was a God sent angel that I needed in this moment. She admitted she made and still make mistakes, but she trusts in God to help guide her in all her daily affairs. She lives life and she isn't waiting to be happy.

We talked about a few more things and she suggested, I learn to forgive myself and make peace with my past, so I can be free in the present. She was so full of wisdom and everything she encouraged me to do, I made up in my mind that I will do just that. We hugged and shared goodbyes and I left her and the luncheon feeling refreshed, my time was now, and I was ready to live.

It's been about five months after the Luncheon with Ms. Sandra, and I was diligently working on my own healing. In between being a mother and running my business. I made sure to make time for myself. I started reading the personal development books given to me by Ms. Sandra.

They taught me a lot. Over the years there were times I couldn't stop crying behind David and there were times I couldn't cry because I needed to be strong for my children. I gave a lot and was given little in return. I was there for people who spit in my face.
I gave up the best years of my life for toxic love.

My breakthrough came one night when I was lounging around the house alone watching a movie. I was feeling a little emotional as I started to think about my life and all the wrong I did, how I lived wrong and loved wrong.

I could no longer focus on the movie because tears were pouring down my eyes.
I blamed myself for many years, on the outside I seemed put together, but I blamed myself for a lot. I lived with regret and I wish I never gave

my heart to a man like David. In some of the books I read they talk about forgiveness and making peace with yourself about your past.

I climbed out of the bed and grabbed a notebook and went inside of my closet and I began to write. I started to write down all the feelings I had about myself over the years and the things I did wrong and allowed. I wrote down the ways I could be accountable to myself and my past and that I was ready to forgive myself and I was ready to let go of the past so I could move forward free.

I began to write a letter to my father, expressing to him how losing his love left an impact on me. I wrote in the letter that if he had been present emotionally then maybe David's love wouldn't have seemed so appealing. I let it all out in those letters.

I wrote one for Paul, because I needed to make peace with that. For a couple of years, hate rested in my heart for my brother because of all the under handed things he's done to me and my family.

When my dad became distant, it was Paul who stepped up for me and to think he would be the one to destroy me and my children's lives.

I would have never thought it would be my own flesh and blood, my blood brother with who I shared the same mother and father. His love for money turned his heart cold and ever since he fell in love with money, he would do anything to acquire it even if that meant hurting his own flesh and blood. I let everything out in that letter, and I may a vow to let go of the hate for Paul.

I don't know if we would ever reconcile and be like we were but that night I decided to just love my brother from a distance.

I also wrote a letter to my dear aunt, who I loved dearly, and I felt like I let her down over the years. I felt like this wouldn't have been the life I lived if she hadn't been taken from me. After knowing she suffered from domestic violence, I felt bad that I accepted in my life. I let her know that I was going to do better from here on out. I wanted her to be proud of me. I let her know I missed her and that I'm going to make peace in knowing she was taken away from me and I will let the hate that I have for her ex, go. I cried all night, I was so heavy and because I carried it well, no one knew. I needed this moment to release some things from my heart and from my mind. I need to release these things for my healing. I realized that my healing isn't a one-time thing but a journey and each stride I make, I'm getting better. In the middle of my breakthrough, my phone rings.

I ignore it the first couple of times but when this person called a third time, I decided to answer the phone and low and behold it was Trice crying in my ear.

"What's going on girl?" I asked trying to get myself together so she wouldn't hear the sadness in my voice.
"Girl, Ahmad is fucked up girl, this nigga is fucked up, girl I can't believe after everything I fucking did for him, he would do me this way!" She yelled quickly into the receiver.

"Hold on, slow down, what happened now?"
"So, you know every time he starts cheating, he starts acting differently, well so he was on that bullshit again. Taking his phone everywhere, he changed his passcode, he been staying out late and we been only having sex like once a fucking week. So, I know his ass is cheating on me.
One night he gets a phone call and I overhear him tell the person that he was on the way, that motherfucker didn't know I could hear him.

He took a shower, got dressed and left. I gave it like two minutes, and I slipped on my shoes and followed him in my car. I stayed close on his ass, and he was so thirsty for some ass that he didn't even realize I was tailing him. His ass so trifling, he got a good ass educated woman yet his ass still going to the hood for ghetto ass girls. He pulls up to this raggedy ass house and a nigga come out, they dap each other up and they go in the house. He stayed

 in there for a about an hour or two because my ass waited but nothing happened, so I went home. The next couple of nights, I followed him over to this same house. I let a few days pass by and figured maybe he was just kicking with some new niggas until a bitch got access to his phone my nosey ass had to peek over his shoulder to get that code. I go in his phone

 into his text messages and this nigga got about three threads of text messages from niggas and this nasty, trifling ass motherfucker was getting these men to send him dick pics and one even sent him a video of them having sex and it was that same man he was going to go see every night. I literally threw up in my mouth.

 I fucked him up that night, it was one thing to be fucking other bitches but my nigga fucking other men I can't do, I felt like I couldn't compete with some of those other bitches, how am I supposed to compete with a fucking man! Lauren what the fuck did I do to deserve this, I gave him everything, even almost fucked up being partner behind this man. Paid for things for him. I gave him every fucking thing!"

"Damn, Trice, I am so sorry girl, I don't even know what to say, that's messed up girl."
"Man, fuck him, Lauren I put up with a lot from him, thought he would change for me and he still shit on me, I threw all his shit out and put his ass out in the middle of the night. I'm tired girl, I'm so damn tired. I make too much money and I'm too damn old to be tryna get these niggas to do right, what you doing, girl I need to get out of this house, I can still smell him and it's pissing me off."

"Yea, you can come over, I could use the company too."

Trice came over and she cried, and we cried together. We both had a breakthrough that night in different ways. I think she is starting to realize that she can't buy love from these men and that sex won't keep them faithful either. I gave her a couple of the books

Ms.Sandra gave me and hopefully she will learn to love herself too.

That night I slept the best I had slept in years, it definitely feels different when you let go of dead weight and find the peace God intended for us to have.

Chapter 8

The Lauren Prayer

The past few months have been the best months I've had in a while. I was loving myself in a way I never knew. My mind was clear, and I had this new aura about myself that even others around me could pick up on. Self-Love was all around me. I exuded a level of confidence that when I walked in a room, I lit it up. I was always a go-getter and I knew how to make a way out of no way but the love I had for myself made me a whole new woman. My birthday was coming up and the girls and I were planning a trip to D.C, little did I know this trip to D.C would change my life forever. 2016 was a year, I'd never forget.Shermaine, Trice, Ms.Sandra and myself arrived in D.C and we were ready to party. All of us had so much going on in our lives, I was so happy that they were able to make time for me.

Shermaine left her husband due to his constant infidelities, she could no longer deal with all his baby mamas and his outside children. Shermaine always depended on a man financially, she loved being a sugar baby but after everything she went through with her husband, she was ready to do for herself. She recently received her Real Estate License. Her plans are to sell and flip homes. I was happy for her, all her life she had a man in the pocket to take care of her and now that she was following a dream she had before she started stripping. It was good to see her in this space. Trice finally cut Ahmad loose, she finally made the decision to let him go.

After catching him with men, she stayed around a few more months being fed lies about him changing but she kept catching him with other women and men. She reached her breaking point, and she left him, and it seems as if she hasn't looked back. She channeled that energy into her career, and she finally made Partner at her law firm. Although she was progressing career wise, Trice still found herself out partying like she was twenty-five years old and messing with young boys.

Ms. Sandra was back dating again and she met a lovely man who adored her.
She was just so sweet, and it was nice to see her with a companion.

Shermaine and Trice planned a party for me at one of the local lounges in D.C. I hired a local makeup and hair stylist to make sure I looked beautiful that night. I lost a few pounds so the little black dress I brought hugged my curves in all the right places. We took a few celebratory shots of liquor and we made our way downstairs to head over to the lounge.

Once we arrived at the lounge it was busy and packed. Shermaine led us over to our own private table and the fun had just began. The music was flowing, and I was having a great time dancing with the girls when this fine dark-skinned brother approached me at the table.

"How are you? My name is Jermaine, you look beautiful tonight." He said into my ear over the loud music. "What's your name? Where are you from?

"My name is Lauren, I'm from North Carolina. What about you?"

"You won't believe this but I'm from North Carolina myself. I'm up in D.C on business. What brings you to the city'?"

"Oh whatever, you're not from North Carolina?" I said jokingly.

"I promise you I am." he said as he pulled out his wallet to show me his state ID.

"Oh, I guess are you." I said with a smirk. "Oh we're here celebrating my birthday?"

"Happy Birthday to you beautiful."

I introduced him to my girls, and I invited him to sit over with us at the table. We talked a bit more and then we exchanged numbers and he said he would call me some time over the weekend. He was so fine, he smelled so good and he had a smile that made you want to have his babies. I continued to enjoy my party, but I couldn't help but think about fine ass Jermaine.
The weekend had come and gone and D.C was everything. From the party at the Lounge, to the spa day, to dinner at fancy restaurants, to Jermaine taking me to breakfast. I enjoyed

my thirty-eighth birthday.

It's been a few months and I was having the best time of my life. Everything that I prayed for was manifesting right before my eyes. Damian was still successful in his business. Destiny was in college pursing her nursing degree. My childcare centers were five-star centers and I was gaining so much clientele that I had to establish a waiting list for both centers. Business was doing so well; I was in the process of opening a third center. I had money before.

David and I made tons of money together, but the money only made our life better for a moment and we were back having problems. The more money he and I had; the more problems came but this time was different. I made a lot of money for myself, but I didn't let that money change me or become a problem in my life. I learned how to invest and make my money work for me and not become a problem in my life.

Since D.C Jermaine became a great friend to me. He lived in Raleigh and he came to visit me every other weekend and we talked on the phone every day. He was different than the men I was used to dating. He was kind and compassionate and a man of his word. He listened to me and he valued me as a woman. He was successful in his business, but he wasn't driven by money and I loved that about him.

I found myself thinking about Jermaine daily, but I was scared to take it further due to some trust issues I had within. He would often let me know his intent and I let him know that I liked him, but I wanted to take things slow and he was patient with me. He continued to make time for me and through his actions and words he was intentional about the way he showed he cared for me.

Late August of 2016, Jermaine planned a weekend trip for us down in Atlanta. We flew separately and planned to meet at the hotel. When I arrived at the room, he opened the door, I could see candles lit all over the room and rose petals led from the door into the suite.

Before I could walk in, we shared a kiss that sent chills down my spine. He grabbed my bags and took me by the hand and led me inside. He set me at the table which was surrounded by candles and dinner.
He went to put my bags into the bedroom and came back and pulled me up on my feet and planted another kiss on my lips.

He had the sexiest lips. We kissed a little longer this time. Up until this point Jermaine and I have only shared kisses, but I was dying to feel him inside of me.

A part of me wanted to skip right past dinner so I can have him for dessert and maybe he felt my energy because the kisses didn't stop, and I found his hand moving down my spine and on top of my ass. The faucet between my legs was turned on and flowing. He took me by the hand, and we went into the bedroom. He went all out, there was candles and rose petals everywhere.

He laid me down on the bed and he unbuttoned my dress and threw it on the floor next was my bra and my panties. He began to kiss me from head to toe. He stopped and gave my breast a little love and I was gushing, water flowed out of my body.

He made his way between my legs and gave my honey spot some love and it was everything that I could have imagined. We continued engaging in foreplay and both of us was ready for more. He slipped on a condom and enter the wet parts of me, and we made love, it was passionate, it was intense, it was deeper than just the physical act, this was an emotional connection for the both of us.

We made love until the sun came up and once we were done, we rested in each other's arms and the feeling of peace and love covered us.

Jermaine treated me like royalty, the entire weekend. I was tired of getting the short end of the stick when it came to men. During my quiet time alone, I started to be proactive in my prayers. I would often recite the Serenity Prayer which became my favorite prayer. I prayed to become a better woman for myself and for my next relationship.

I became more specific about the type of man I wanted in my life. I wanted to be loved the right way and he showed me that in every way. I prayed for a man that accepted me for who I was, my flaws and all. I prayed for a man who I could be free and comfortable with. I prayed for a man who values and honors me. I prayed for a man who would accept that I am a mother and I have two children who I love. I prayed for a man who was successful but wasn't in love with money. I prayed for a man who was patient, who could lead and who was responsible. He was a man who thought of me outside of his self. I prayed for Jermaine. He was the answer to my prayer.

Chapter 9

One of a kind Love

It's been about a year since Jermaine and I have met, and things were still progressing with us. We were officially a couple and decided to build a life together. He proposed to me at his friend's New Year's Eve party and we planned to get married in September. Jermaine was a blessing to have, my children loved him, and he loved my children.

I was married before, but this time was going to be different. He said I could have my dream wedding and that was the wedding we planned. The only things I stressed about was if I was going to invite my father.

Jermaine encouraged me to rebuild that relationship and over the past few months we've had several intense phone conversations and I went to see him a couple of times. I also brought the children along.

Things weren't perfect but we were making progress to rebuild our father and daughter relationship. Jermaine knew of my feelings of being rejected by him, but he still encouraged me to invite him. I sent him an invitation and I left it in God's hands.

The day finally arrived, and everything was perfect. I was nervous but I was grateful at the same time. God restored everything that I lost over the years back to me. He gave me love, joy, peace and contentment. He showed me how to love myself and in return I was blessed to have a man that loves me the way God loves me.

When I look back at the life and love I shared with David I realized that wasn't love or the way to live. It was toxic and it was all wrong. The best thing that happened from that relationship was our children. David isn't a horrible man, he just wasn't the man I needed in my life.

When I think about who I'm about to see at the end of the aisle, I can't help but smile. Jermaine is that one of a kind love, that love most people could only dream about.

My mother helped me slip on my shoes, my makeup artist applied some final touches to my lipstick. I stood up to walk towards the door and I see my father there, dressed in his tux and tears instantly fell from my eyes. God not only restored my faith in love, he restored my relationship with my father. We shared a hug and he kissed me on the cheek. My mother wiped the tears from my face. My parents grabbed a hand each and we walked out of the room and it was time I married my one of a kind love.

The wedding was perfect. Our theme was a night in Paris. Everything was white with touches of pink. The ceiling was decorated with string lights that represented a starry night. We also had our own Eiffel tower erected in the rear of the venue.

We danced to *Fall for you by Leela James* as I imagined being on the streets of Paris with the man I love. He held me close and I could feel his heartbeat and I knew we were going to be connected forever. In that moment I felt like Heaven came to earth.

I was on cloud 9 and the icing on the cake was when he surprised me and told me Paris was the place we were going for our Honeymoon. This man knew how to make me smile. A love that I thought only existed in fairy tales was now a love I've been fortunate to behold. I was now Mrs. Jermaine Davis and I was ready to see what God had in store for us and our family.

■■■

"Push!" the nurses and my mother scream in unison as I squeeze Jermaine's hand as I give birth to our son.

"Give us one last push!" the doctor said as I could feel my son's head crowning.

Tears seeped from my eyes as they pulled my son out and laid him on my chest. Our son was born July 12th, 2018. Jermaine kissed me on the lips and then proceeded to kiss our son. I was happy to be his wife but to solidify our union with our son was everything.

We named him after Jermaine because this was his first child and first son, and I knew that would mean so much to him.

My heart was overjoyed, I would have never thought I would have this life, but God redeemed my time.

After we had JJ, we settle into family life. We had a few challenges, but we were able to work through them in a way that I've never experienced. In the past I was used to shouting and arguing to make a point but with Jermaine, I didn't have to do all of that to be heard. Although our relationship was healthy, I never stopped learning and growing. I continued to better myself so I could be a better woman, wife and mother.

I finally graduated from college with my degree in business. To have my children, the man I loved and my mom present to see me walk across the stage, meant the world to me. After graduation Jermaine and I went into business together, opening a group home and a non-profit for trouble youth. He was once a troubled teenager and he wanted to show them that life doesn't have to end the way it started. He was passionate about the group home and non-profit and I was grateful to be by his side.

Jermaine did everything with purpose. He made sure to include my family in a lot of the things we did. He took our family on vacations. We went to Disney World in Florida, we went to see the Walk of Fame in L.A, and we even went Skiing in Aspen, Colorado.

My favorite Trip was when we took the family to Puerto Rico, it was everyone's first time out of the country, so it was special to me. When we weren't traveling, we would have family and friends over at the house. Jermaine loved entertaining, he loved being surrounded by our children, our family and our friends. I was so happy to be with this man. I was at peace with him. His love came at the right time and I was blessed to have the love of God in human form.

Chapter 10

Living and Loving Right

Many of us live and love wrong and for most of us that's all we know based upon what we've seen as children. As we grow, if we don't learn better, we begin to imitate those same behaviors in our own life by the people we fall in "love" with and by the type of life we choose to live. I was living and loving wrong for years, while my parents did the best they could, their behaviors and the things I seen from others around me drew me closer to choosing the wrong life and the wrong partner.

Everything I went through put me where I am now. Those lessons helped me see that living and loving wrong wasn't how I want to spend my time here on earth.

So, I began to invest in myself and my own personal development. A relationship with God and self-love are necessary in order to rise out of dysfunction. When I began to grow spiritually and love myself that's when I began to live and love right. It all goes hand in hand, without God or self-love you won't live or love right.

I remember pulling into the driveway of the home I share with my husband and our son. A tear fell down my eyes and I began to thank God to finally be in this place. My life isn't perfect and I'm still growing but I'm far from the life I use to live. It's easy to live wrong but it takes self-discipline, self-control, accountability and honesty to live and love right and most people aren't willing to do those things to be successful in their life.

I made the decision to turn my life around and it's possible for anyone to do it. I was a teen mother in a abusive relationship with a man I loved, a man I let cheat on me and destroy my self-esteem and self-worth.

We were living a lifestyle that brought in tons of money, but it was a lifestyle that had us ducking the cops and making sure we were on our p's and q's at all times.

Even though we had tons of money, with that type of life, the more money we had the more problems came our way. There were good moments during those years, but I spent a lot of those years, depressed, stressed and feeling worthless. I thought love meant pain and that when you love someone you suppose to accept any and everything from them,but that's not love. Love isn't toxic, love doesn't destroy. Love grows, Love is patient, Love makes you better, Love is self-less. I was able to overcome; I was able to rise the dysfunction.

I was able to learn how to love my children better, instead of giving them everything they desired materially and not holding them accountable for their actions. I began to give them things they wanted when they showed me, they could handle the responsibility. I wanted them to know that as their mother I would always love them but also as their mother I must hold them accountable and I also must teach them that there are consequences for their actions and that I may not always be there to bail them out.

They became better for themselves and they began to make healthier decisions that will help them live and love right. Damian although he started going down the wrong path, when he was younger, my son made a complete 180 and he is engaged to be married to a beautiful woman who the family loves. He learned that he didn't want to get rich the wrong way because he didn't want to end up in the feds being able to only spend three hundred dollars a month. Damian didn't want that life, he wanted to make legit money and he wanted his freedom. He also just purchased his first home and his business is doing so well that he is planning to open another one.

Destiny graduated from nursing school and is now working as an RN at a hospital in Raleigh, NC. She is also in the process of purchasing her own home. She has become one of my best friends. She comes down often to visit us. She is currently single and her focus in the moment is her career and life. Damian and Destiny are still praying for their dad to be home.

J.J is growing up beautifully, it's nice to raise a child in a home where he doesn't have to hide in his room because of the constant yelling or fighting.

He is a happy child, and I don't have to overcompensate to show him my love.

My relationship with my father is still a work in progress. We talk often and he has even come out to some of the functions we've had at our home. I am happy to be in this place and I will forever be grateful to him for being there for me at my wedding. He interacts with his grandchildren and J.J gets to have his grandpa in his life. I haven't spoken to my brother Paul, but I made peace with that decision. Some family you have to love from a distance. I don't carry anymore hate in my heart for him, but I must protect my peace by keeping my distance. My mom tried to get us to reconcile but after the last attempt. She understands my position in it all. I love my brother I always will but until he's ready to live and love right, he must remain out of my life.

My friends have also moved towards the journey of living and loving right. We brought Ms. Sandra in as our Nanny for J.J she is the best person to trust with my son. She is still with her man and they plan to marry soon. She has always had the keys to living and loving right and I'm glad I could learn from her.

Trice isn't quite there yet but she's making progress towards getting it right. She isn't giving her money away to men or taking care of them like she used to, but she still entertains some men that aren't the best for her. I know she will get there as I could see small changes in her. It's only a matter of time before Trice is living and loving right.

Shermaine also did a complete 180, my best friend who use to use men and strip to make ends meet, is now a mother and the owner of her own Real Estate Agency and she is buying up the city. I could see it in her eyes the way she loves herself, she's glowing and it's nice to see her on the journey to living and loving right.

As for me, I am still a work in progress and a beautiful masterpiece. I took a lot of pain over the years and I've shed a lot of tears. I've been down and I haven't always lived right or loved right. I've been through countless storms. I have overcome, and I am able to still stand. God restores, he redeems, your only job is to trust in him, and his plan and he'll make your latter days better than your former days.

I am standing here today a changed woman who finally got it. It's never too late to make the change and to get things right in your life. If I can do it, if I can finally free myself from living and loving wrong, you have the the power to do it too.

Life's Treasures

What's for you will not be toxic or messy

I pray you heal from things no one ever apologizes for

There is a message in the way people treat you

Make room for people who want to love you

Don't block your blessing by trying to treat people how they treat you

Sometimes we forget who we are, just sit back and whoosah

Patience is a virtue

All is fair in love and war

There is light on the other side of the tunnel, remember you may go through more than one tunnel so darkness may come more than once but it will eventually be light

You are free to choose but you are not free from the consequences of your choices

The Three C's of Life: Choices, Chances, Changes

Living and Loving Wrong

Stephanie Diane

www.ingramcontent.com/pod-product-compliance
Lightning Source LLC
Chambersburg PA
CBHW030146200626
46812CB00015B/1726